ROBIN HOOD

WILL YOU TOLERATE THIS?

BBC CHILDREN'S BOOKS

Published by the Penguin Group
Penguin Books Ltd, 80 Strand, London WC2R 0RL, England
Penguin Group (USA) Inc., 375 Hudson Street, New York, New York 10014, USA
Penguin Group (Australia) Ltd, 250 Camberwell Road, Camberwell, Victoria, 3124, Australia
(a division of Pearson Australia Group Pty Ltd)
Canada, India, New Zealand, South Africa

Published by BBC Children's Books, 2006

3

Text and design © BBC Children's Character Books, 2006
Images © Tiger Aspect Productions 2006
BBC & logo © and ™ BBC 1996
Robin Hood logo ™ and © Tiger Aspect Productions 2006. Licensed by BBC Worldwide Ltd.

All rights reserved.

ISBN 978 1 405 90318 9

Printed in the United Kingdom

ROBIN HOOD

WILL YOU TOLERATE THIS?

Adapted by Kirsty Neale from the television script "Will You Tolerate This?" by Dominic Minghella for the television series Robin Hood created by Dominic Minghella and Foz Allan for Tiger Aspect as shown on BBC One.

CHAPTER ONE

Will You Tolerate This?

'This way,' Robin of Locksley called over his shoulder, pounding through the thickening greenery of the forest. He could still hear the horse's hooves a short way ahead, and the occasional glimpse of the rider's black cloak was enough to let him know they were going in the right direction.

'I'm dying,' panted Robin's manservant and companion, Much, who was trailing behind.

Pausing for a moment, Robin put out an arm to hold him back. The horse had drawn to a stop and as they stood and listened, other sounds drifted through the forest towards them.

'You know the law,' came a cold, hard voice.

'I know the law is an ass,' a second man answered.

Much smirked.

Glancing around, Robin moved towards the trunk of a broad oak tree and beckoned for his friend to follow.

'The price for one of the King's deer is your right hand,' said the first voice again.

Robin peered out from behind the oak's solid trunk, and through a gap in the dense thicket saw the grubby, fair-haired man who had run across their path a short while before. Two of the uniformed Sheriff's men were binding his arms and legs. A third man, still mounted, watched over them. Robin guessed he was in charge.

'No!' cried the man. 'Please, have mercy. My wife expects a child, and we have no food. She must eat or she will lose the baby.'

Silently, and with a growing feeling of unease, Robin adjusted his bow and pulled three arrows from the quiver on his back. He was beginning to fear things in England had changed greatly in the five years he and Much had been away, and not for the better.

'We can punish you now,' the chief Sheriff's

man said as his prisoner began to wail again. 'If you admit your guilt and save us time, the punishment is lessened. We can take a finger, but you will have no right to trial. No defence, no appeal.'

'I will lose a trial.' The man considered. 'And my hand,' he finished.

There was a grim pause.

'Take the finger,' he said.

Beside Robin, Much fidgeted. He was only half-listening to what was going on in the clearing ahead.

'Why must you always pick such wet hiding places?' he hissed, rubbing his hand irritably over a grass-dampened patch on the seat of his trousers.

Robin didn't answer.

Just twenty minutes ago, sulked Much, he'd felt positively cheerful. A song in his heart, if not – thanks to Robin's protestations – on his lips, and a head filled with delicious dreams of the feast that awaited them back at Locksley.

His stomach growled again at the memory. Beef, pig, lamb. After months of travelling, they were so close to home, surely no more than a day's walk from the village. And then this dirt-stained, deer-hunting peasant had streaked across the path in front of them, closely followed by a dozen of the Sheriff's meanest-looking henchmen. Robin had quizzed the last of them about the peasant's crime.

'He'll lose a hand,' the weaselly man had told them.

Much's instincts had suggested they run in the opposite direction, but Robin's had led them into the forest after the Sheriff's men and the needy stranger. Knowing his master as he did, Much supposed he should not have been surprised. It wasn't as if he didn't sympathise with the hunter; the thought of roast deer was enough to make Much almost faint with hunger. He just couldn't see what the whole sorry situation had to do with him.

In the clearing, two of the Sheriff's men

dragged their prisoner to a gnarled tree stump. One of them was brandishing a small axe, its blade glinting dangerously in the dim, filtered forest light.

Robin sensed it was almost time to act. He pulled a handful of stones from a small pouch tied at his waist and passed them to Much. 'You know what to do.'

Much nodded.

'Put your hand on here,' one of the Sheriff's men told the squirming prisoner. 'Like this,' he added, spreading his own hand flat on the tree stump to demonstrate.

Robin slipped out from behind the oak tree and readied his bow.

'No!' the prisoner wailed again. 'I've changed my mind.'

'No appeal,' mocked the Sheriff's man.

Robin took aim.

The first three arrows landed neatly between the splayed fingers of the Sheriff's man, their points sinking into the wooden stump in quick succession and with a series of satisfying thwacks.

'What the – ?'

Two more arrows pierced the bewildered henchman's cuff and fixed it firmly to the wood of the stump.

'Who's there?' he demanded.

'It seems I missed your hand.' Robin raised his voice, but didn't yet reveal himself. 'Let him go before my aim improves.'

'Show yourself,' demanded the chief Sheriff's man. 'You interfere with the law of the land.'

Robin pulled up his hood and stepped forward. Still in his hiding place, Much began to throw the stones so they thudded around the edges of the clearing. The chief Sheriff's man glanced around, and Robin knew that he had mistaken the sound of the stones for footfalls. As far as the chief was concerned, he and his men were surrounded by a band of outlaws, just as Robin had planned.

'Last time I looked,' Robin said, 'the law punished poaching with a tanning or a spell in the stocks.'

'Then you've been away,' the Sheriff's man said flatly. 'These are rotten times. The law is under threat and must be severe if it is to be respected.'

'If the law wants respect, shouldn't the punishment fit the crime?'

Robin was pleased to see the Sheriff's man falter.

'I do not make the law. I do not decide.'

'But you enforce it. That is a decision.' Robin heard more of Much's stones landing and rustling the leaves around them. 'My men and I suggest you decide to go on your way, and let this man feed his hungry wife.'

'I don't know...'

The Sheriff's man hesitated, and Robin pulled a fresh arrow from his quiver.

'You know,' he said, firing it up into the air above them.

'What does that prove?' The Sheriff's man scoffed, as the arrow vanished.

Robin waited.

A moment later, dropping from the sky

nose-down and perfectly straight, the arrow landed in the saddle of the chief's horse. It narrowly missed the chief himself. Around the clearing, the Sheriff's men gasped.

'Missed again,' said Robin, raising his eyebrows in mock exasperation.

There was an uncomfortable silence, and then the chief nodded to his men. With a small flurry of movement and ropes, the prisoner was released.

'God bless you sir,' he said, looking directly at Robin.

'Come,' interrupted the chief Sheriff's man, 'we leave these rogues to their crime.'

Taking their orders, the men began to follow him. Robin turned back to the released prisoner, but was surprised to see he had vanished.

'Us, rogues?' came a voice from the edge of the clearing.

Obviously emboldened by the success of their plan, Much had stepped out from his hiding place. Robin's heart sank.

'Don't show your faces here again, cowards,'

Much told the departing Sheriff's men.

'Quiet,' warned Robin.

'Why? We have won and they should be ashamed.' Much was clearly getting carried away. 'Shame on you,' he shouted after the Sheriff's men. 'May God strike you with unpleasant pains. May girls laugh when they see you naked. Come back here another time and my master and I will see that you leave with more than just your tails between your legs.'

Robin smacked a hand against his forehead and apparently the chief Sheriff's man realised what Much had said at the same moment.

'My master and I?' he echoed. Just the two of you? Robin could almost hear him thinking.

'I shouldn't have said that,' groaned Much and almost as quickly as the prisoner had done, the two of them disappeared into the forest, pounding once again through the thick foliage with the sound of hooves ringing in their ears.

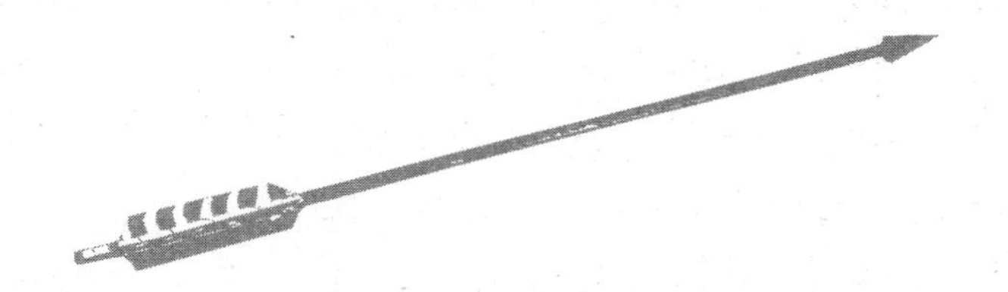

CHAPTER TWO

Will You Tolerate This?

Much supposed he deserved it as he struggled to keep up with Robin, branches scratching and pulling at his clothes. Why couldn't he just have kept his mouth shut? The Sheriff's men were close and shouting behind them. Much didn't want to think about what would happen if they caught up with him. He wasn't keen on the idea of living out his days as a nine-fingered man. As he tore through a fresh tangle of bushes, he realised with a jolt of panic that Robin had disappeared from view. His eyes strained in the gloomy green light for any sign of movement ahead as his ears tried to block out the advancing yells from behind. Without warning, something caught his ankle and stifling a scream, Much fell forwards. The something that had caught his ankle gave a second sharp tug and pulled him backwards. Much turned his head and saw that it was Robin. They were crammed beneath an enormous log and his master had grabbed Much just in time. Above them, horses were crashing through the undergrowth and one after another their hooves soared over the log. Exhausted and grateful yet again for Robin's quick thinking, Much lay still and silent on the damp earth until the sounds of the mounted Sheriff's men died away.

'Clever, Master –' he began, making to move out from their tight and uncomfortable hiding place.

But Robin clamped a hand firmly over his mouth, and before Much had a chance to protest his indignation, the reason became clear. One final horse appeared above them. Much froze and beside him felt Robin do the same. Instead of following their fellows, the horse and its uniformed rider were circling around just inches from the fallen log. The hooves stopped for a moment and then, to Much's horror, the ugly face of the Sheriff's man peered straight at them.

'I can see you,' he said in a sing-song voice.

Robin silently prepared an arrow.

Much felt a trickle of chilly sweat run down his back.

The face stared for a few more moments, and then disappeared. As he heard the horse finally moving away, Much let out a proper breath for what felt like the first time since they'd left the clearing. The Sheriff's man had been bluffing. Much's fingers were safe, for the time being at least.

'Five years in battle,' Robin berated as they scrambled out from beneath the log, 'and you still forget the last man.'

'There is so much to remember,' grumbled Much quietly.

Their run-in with the Sheriff's men greatly concerned Robin, and he was mostly silent as they returned to the path and continued home to Locksley. Something just didn't feel right about the way those men had treated the hunter. To lose a finger and not even be granted a proper trial or right to defend himself - how had the law come to such a state? The more Robin considered, the more unsettled he felt.

Beside him, Much was also silent and Robin was grateful. After five years together in battle his friend had learned to sense when Robin needed to be quiet, to mull over his thoughts without interruption. There was also, Robin acknowledged, the possibility that Much's silence was due in some small part to sulking over his having forgotten about the last man.

By mid-afternoon, however, Robin's unease began to subside. The sun was warm above them and Much returned to talk of food and song and home. Robin's spirits were further lifted when the path they were following led them past the yard of a fullery. Dyed bolts of cloth hung all around, waving and billowing as they dried in the late spring breeze. To Robin, it was a sight that reminded him of the old Nottingham. Maybe things had not changed so much after all.

As they walked past, Robin saw that the fuller was digging a fresh ditch in the yard. He paused to wipe the sweat off his forehead and caught sight of Robin and Much.

'You two on the run?' asked the fuller, one hand still on his spade.

'We are returning to Locksley after a long absence,' said Robin.

'You look like you're on the run,' he grunted, but Robin hardly heard him. He had just noticed a girl. A very pretty girl. He suspected she was the fuller's daughter and he was fairly certain she'd noticed him, too.

'...want to help with this ditch?' the fuller was now saying. 'There's a good meal in it. We have a pork roasting.'

Unsurprisingly, it was Much who answered, thinking as usual with his stomach. 'Master, we could, couldn't we?'

'We are nearly home.'

'I know, but pork – pork would be...' Much's anguished, pleading, always-hungry voice trailed away.

'Very well,' Robin relented. 'You shall have pork.'

'Really?' said Much, amazed. 'I love you. Have I ever said that?'

Robin grinned. As keen as he was to get home, he had to admit a short stay at the fullery had its attractions. Unlike Much, it was not dinner that was on Robin's mind.

'October ale?' said a female voice a short while later. Robin and Much looked up from their almost-finished ditch, sweating and dirty. It was the girl Robin had spotted earlier and she was carrying a large earthenware pitcher.

'Thank you,' said Robin as she handed him the ale. He took a grateful swig. 'What is your name?'

'Sarah.'

'You and your ale are a welcome sight for toiling men, Sarah.' Robin looked directly into her eyes, and she held his gaze.

'Please,' said Much, darkly.

Robin was about to snap at him, when the

fuller returned. He wandered up and down the ditch, appraising their work and then, apparently satisfied, nodded at Sarah.

'Bring out the food.'

'May I help?' said Robin, spotting an opportunity. And before Sarah had a chance to answer, he followed her into the fullery.

She bustled about, covering the pitcher of ale and attending to the roast pork, which even Robin had to admit, smelled delicious. It wasn't enough to distract him from a woman this beautiful, however.

He leaned against the solid wooden table gazing at her.

'Sarah, you have eyes that –'

'What?' she said, looking up at him.

'Seem to see right into me,' Robin said. 'I believe you can read my mind.'

'What makes you say that?'

'I think you can see my hopes, my dreams...' Robin moved closer as he spoke and inclined his head towards her, 'my desires.'

But rather than leaning in to kiss him as he

had hoped – it was, after all, a speech which had worked out that way many times before – Sarah moved away. Robin frowned. She didn't seem uncomfortable, quite the opposite in fact, but he couldn't read the look on her face. As he watched, she picked up a bolt of fabric from the drying rack and pulled it across the open window behind them. He caught a brief glimpse of her father before the cloth swung into place and suddenly realised what she was doing. Shielded from view, Sarah grabbed him and just a few seconds later than Robin had planned, she kissed him.

CHAPTER THREE

'It is as deep as you wanted,' Much told the fuller as they surveyed the ditch.

'I don't want it at all,' said the fuller, picking up Robin's discarded shovel and stabbing it into the earth. 'I don't want more water. I don't want to dye more cloth.'

Much was confused.

'Sheriff wants cloth dyed for his men. In lieu of taxes,' explained the fuller. 'Taxes I cannot pay because nobody has money to buy my cloth.'

Much nodded, only half-listening. He thought he could smell the pork. He glanced towards the fullery, wondering what was keeping Sarah and Robin. As he watched, a piece of cloth slid from one of the windows revealing a scene which it was definitely best the fuller didn't see. He had a feeling that the sight of Robin and

Sarah kissing would put paid to the promise of roast pork, ditch or no ditch. Panicking, he cast around for something to say, hoping to distract Sarah's father.

'He is a fair-minded old man,' Much said, steering their conversation back to the Sheriff. 'If you explain your difficulties, if you kiss him.' His eyes flickered back to the window. 'Kiss him...' he repeated, panic-stricken.

'Kiss him?' Now it was the fuller's turn to look confused.

Much dragged his gaze away from Robin and Sarah, and pulled himself together. 'Kiss his ring, he will understand. Show respect. Pay allegiance.'

The fuller raised an eyebrow.

'You really have been away. The old man is finished. We've had a new Sheriff these last four years.' He threw a glance in the direction Sarah had gone, luckily not turning far enough round to catch sight of the fullery window. 'Where is that food?'

Much had not been listening, busy instead

willing Robin to leave Sarah alone and think of their roast pork. But now, the fuller's mention of food brought him back to his senses.

'Really?' he said, loudly, in a desperate attempt to carry on the conversation and stop Sarah's father looking back at the fullery. 'Tell me more about that because like I say, he is a fair-minded old man.'

'I told you. We have a new, younger...' The fuller looked at Much suspiciously. 'You're not listening to me.'

And before Much could do anything about it, he turned round to see what the distraction was.

Shouting, raging, rolling up his sleeves in preparation for a fight – none of these would have surprised Much. As it was, the fuller remained tight-lipped and instead pulled from nowhere an enormous sword. Much gulped.

'Robin!' He tried to shout a warning to his master, but his terrified voice came out as a pathetic squeak. The old man was striding towards the fullery with his sword, and Much had no choice but to follow.

Robin gazed into Sarah's soft green eyes and smiled. There was something special about her, his best lines aside. He leaned in to kiss her again, but a moment later, she froze. Robin opened his eyes. Their lips were still touching, but Sarah was staring transfixed at something over Robin's shoulder. With a sense of impending doom, he turned around. The fuller strode through the door, sword in hand and fury in his face. Anticipating an attack, Robin ducked and rolled nimbly out of the way as the fuller lunged with his sword.

'You picked the wrong man to mess with,' snarled the fuller. 'I did not always work with cloth. I once worked metal, and I have never been beaten with a sword. Not by knight, not by knave.'

'Perhaps because you fight when your opponent has no weapon,' said Robin, confidently. 'Much?'

His manservant struggled through the

door, looking hot and bothered. He scooped up Robin's pack and after what felt like half a lifetime of fumbling inside, threw Robin a stubby knife.

'My sword!' said Robin, exasperated, and Much went back to wrestling with the pack.

'I can't get it out,' he grunted, heaving at the weapon as Sarah's father looked on, smirking.

'He has a sword,' the fuller mocked. 'This will be entertaining.'

'Master!' cried Much in relief as the sword finally came free. He hurled it towards Robin who caught it deftly. Realising that the battle was on, the fuller began a show of his skills, twisting and whirling the sword impressively. There was no doubt that he knew what he was doing, and a man who had not seen battle as Robin had would probably have been intimidated.

'Give up now if you like,' taunted the fuller.

'Impressive,' Robin admitted coolly, 'but in the Holy Land, my man and I saw the Turk, and he was more impressive still. If I may give you an example.'

Robin began to manoeuvre with his sword, slowly at first and then gradually speeding up. He was confident, focussed and in complete control of the complicated display as Sarah and Much looked on admiringly.

'Give up now, if you like,' Robin mimicked.

The fuller hesitated, crestfallen and apparently admitting defeat. 'Take what you will and leave.'

But as Robin let both his sword and his guard drop, the fuller made a fresh charge and this time it was towards Much.

'Much!' Robin shouted, his turn now to give warning. He parried, flinging his sword between the two men. 'Fetch your pack. Run!' he said.

Much did as he was told, saved again and leaving Robin to take on the fuller.

The old man was surprisingly good and Robin found himself almost enjoying the challenge. He attacked and dodged, rolled and parried and within a few moments had the fuller pinned against the wall, sword at his throat. One quick flick of his wrist and the man would be dead. He hesitated, conscious of Sarah watching them. Her father was apparently less concerned, and he took advantage of Robin's hesitation, seizing his chance to retaliate. Suddenly, Robin found himself backed into a corner. With nowhere to go, and the fuller bearing down on him, he dropped his sword and put up a hand in defeat.

'Sir, you have me,' he admitted. 'Allow me a final request.'

'What?' The fuller's sword wavered.

'One last kiss,' said Robin. Without waiting for the fuller to respond, he turned to Sarah, kissed her full on the lips and then stepped back onto the open window ledge. In a single smooth movement, Robin propelled himself backwards, catching a fleeting glimpse of the fuller's surprised face as he performed a perfect somersault in mid-air. Both feet landed squarely on the ground below, where Much was waiting with his pack.

'Why do you do that?' Much shouted at

Robin as they ran from the fullery. 'Why do you always, always do that?'

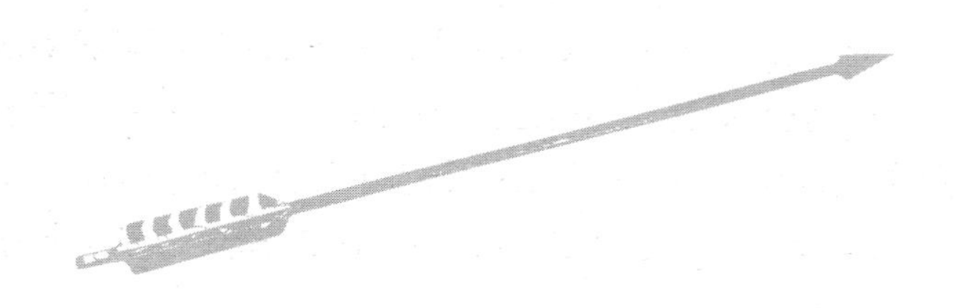

CHAPTER FOUR

Much's stomach rumbled. Thanks to Robin, they had spent another night sleeping in the woods, eating berries and groundnuts instead of their promised pork. The memory of how the roasting meat smelt tortured Much all night. But now, with the midday sun above them, they were nearing home. Locksley lay in the valley below, with the manor and its well-stocked kitchen just beyond. Much fought the urge to sing for joy. From the pensive look on Robin's face, he knew it would be even less appreciated than usual. Instead, he quickened his pace with a little skip, hurrying towards the village – home, and as much pork as he could eat.

It took them less than half an hour to reach

the edge of the village, but even before they got there, Robin had an ominous feeling that something wasn't right. There was a gusting, chilly wind and no sign of villagers on the empty road.

'Where is everyone?' said Much into the silence, as he glanced around.

Robin frowned. There were faces, people in a few of the cottages they passed but they quickly retreated, pulling doors and windows tightly shut behind them.

'Hey, there!' cried Much. Robin followed his gaze and saw an old man by the village water pump. The villager turned to look at the two of them and then, like the other faces Robin had seen, hurried off and disappeared into his cottage.

They're frightened realised Robin as he watched the old man's heavy wooden door slam shut. But of what?

A familiar sound drifted into the silence and interrupted Robin's thoughts. Someone was sawing wood nearby. As he and Much rounded a bend in the road, Robin finally saw a face he knew and it wasn't hiding inside a latched window.

'Dan Scarlett!' he cried, smiling at his old friend.

The carpenter looked up from his sawing.

'Dan? It's me.'

'Robin?'

'Yes!'

Dan scratched his head in amazement. 'Robin? Much? Is it really you?'

'It's us,' Robin assured him. He felt like laughing in relief at having found something – someone – of his old life.

'We are home unscathed,' Much told Dan. 'Well, scathed. Very scathed. But happy. And hungry. Mostly hungry.'

'Blessed Mary, it is you,' said Dan. 'Thank heaven.'

Robin held out his arms and moved to properly greet his friend, but as Dan did the same and they hugged, Robin noticed his left arm. At the end, where his hand had been, was a sealed cuff. No hand. Robin was horrified.

'An accident?' he asked. Surely there could be no other explanation.

'An incident,' said Dan. 'No matter. What's done is done.'

Robin's heart sank. Now he looked more closely at Dan, his hand wasn't the only thing that seemed wrong. It was five years since Robin had last seen him, but Dan's grey hair and drawn features suggested far more time had passed.

'Tell me,' said Robin, afraid of what he was about to hear.

'Guy of Gisborne runs your estate for the Sheriff.' Dan glanced up and for the first time, Robin noticed a guard tower. Two men clad in the same uniform as the Sheriff's men they had met the previous day watched beadily over the village.

'We have one tithe after another for the King in the Holy Land,' Dan continued. 'Making ends meet, it's...' He trailed off, shaking his head in despair. 'It was wrong, but my boys, they took some game. I went to stop them, but so did Gisborne's lot. They were caught. Me, too. Someone had to lose a hand. Better me than Will or little Lukey. I'm old. They have years ahead of them.'

As Dan spoke, Robin's fear turned to anger. 'This is madness,' he said. 'You are a skilled man. You built half this village. I won't have this. You will be compensated. You have my word.'

Dan smiled at him weakly and Robin marvelled at his lack of bitterness.

'I see my boys in good health,' said Dan, as his sons appeared, both a good deal taller than Robin remembered them, 'and I am happy.'

The boys, Luke and Will, were carrying wood for their father, but on seeing him with two strangers, bolted back into the house.

'It's alright,' Dan called after them. 'This is master Robin.'

Luke's face appeared around the edge of the door, his amazement obvious.

'It's alright, Luke.' Robin reassured him.

The boy slipped through the doorway and

made his way nervously towards Robin.

'This is my bow,' he said, showing it off. 'My father made it for me. Why is yours curved?' He was looking at Robin's bow curiously.

'This is a Saracen bow. It is re-curved. See...' Robin demonstrated, and then explained. 'The curves straighten when you draw. Makes it small, but powerful.'

'Is it true you can hit a man a mile away?' said Luke in a rush. 'If I practise every day, I'll be able to do that.'

'Let's hope you never have to shoot a man, Luke.'

'That's what my father says.' Luke tutted. 'I bet you shot hundreds of men alongside the King...?'

Robin smiled, but said nothing.

'Look,' said Luke, undeterred by Robin's reluctance to share his war-stories. He pulled his bow up and aimed an arrow at a small bush beside the cottage.

'Chin higher,' Robin advised. 'And remember to...' Luke fired the arrow, and missed, 'take a breath first.'

'Wait, I'll show you again.' Luke ran to fetch more arrows.

'A credit to you and Jane,' said Robin to Dan.

Dan's face fell and he didn't answer. It took Robin a couple of seconds to realise why.

'No?' he said. Jane couldn't be dead.

Dan nodded. 'Two years,' he said, hoarsely. 'Told us she was eating. Don't think she was. She couldn't see her boys starve. But...' He sighed. 'The whole village has suffered, not just us.'

'Jane? Your good, strong wife?' Robin shook his head in disbelief. It felt as though the world, or at least his piece of it, had been turned upside down and ripped apart in the time he'd been away.

Dan opened his mouth to reply, but they were suddenly disturbed by a commotion a short distance away. Running towards the noise, which was amplified hugely in the quiet, empty village, Robin saw a group of men running into one of the small cottages and just moments later, dragging out the occupants. Sounds coming from inside suggested that they were ransacking the place, searching for something and not caring what they disturbed in the hunt. Looking down on the action from his horse was a man Robin recognised as Guy of Gisborne. As people appeared from nearby houses, screaming and shouting in protest, a slow, satisfied smirk spread across his cruel features.

'Ten sacks of flour have gone missing from the store.' He spoke slowly and clearly to the small crowd below. 'They will be found. They will be accounted for.' His meaning couldn't have been clearer.

Robin saw Much's fingers curl up into his palms.

Behind them, Gisborne's men came out of the house, this time dragging a boy and two sacks of flour. The boy looked no older than fifteen and as Robin watched the men bind him, his expression wavered between fear and defiance.

'No more, sir,' said another of Gisborne's men, coming out of the house.

Guy's displeasure was obvious. 'Who helped this runt?' he demanded. 'Step forward now. I may show lenience.'

No one moved and no one spoke.

'The remaining perpetrators will be found, and this crime will be punished,' spat Gisborne. He turned to his men. 'Bring the boy.'

As he turned to leave, Robin shouted from the back of the crowd. 'Wait!'

He pushed his way forward. 'Guy of Gisborne,' he called again, this time more loudly.

Gisborne turned around. The nearest henchman scowled at Robin.

'Sir Guy of Gisborne to you. And bow before your master.'

Robin bowed, taking just a moment before he spoke again.

'Sir Guy of Gisborne, I am Robin, Earl of Huntingdon and lord of this manor.

Your services here are no longer required.'

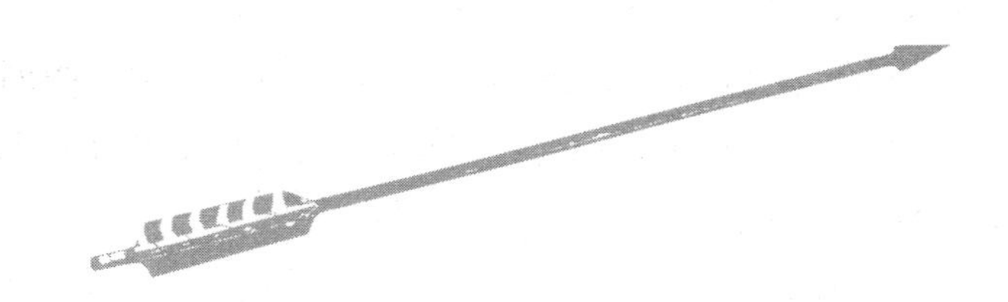

CHAPTER FIVE

'Welcome back, sir,' said Robin's head servant, Thornton, as he strode into Locksley Manor. He turned to a nearby serving girl. 'A bath for the master, Hannah, and fresh clothes immediately.'

'And me, too,' said Much. Robin gazed around the entrance hall, taking in every familiar detail.

Thornton raised an eyebrow. 'Pardon?'

Much looked meaningfully at Robin.

'Thornton, Much is no longer my manservant,' said Robin, taking the hint.

'Oh.'

'In recognition of his service to me in the Holy Land, he is to be a free man. I am granting him the fields and lodge at Bonchurch. Until then, he is a guest in my house.'

'And I would like a plate of something while I bathe.' Much swelled visibly with pride and self-importance.

'Very well,' said Thornton, barely managing to disguise his scorn.

Much lifted his nose into the air and stalked off to bathe.

'That is the way to the servants' quarters,' called Thornton after him.

Without missing a beat, Much changed direction. Head still held high, he continued to stalk, but this time towards the main house.

Robin watched Much enjoying his new-found status in amusement, but his good humour lasted no more than a few seconds. Gisborne and his men had followed them back to the manor.

'Welcome back, Locksley,' said Guy, sweeping through the front door. There wasn't a hint of sincerity in his tone. 'I have kept your lands for you, I have managed your estates to the best of my ability under the guidance of the Sheriff, and I would appreciate more respect in front

of the populace.'

'How many years have you been here?' asked Robin.

'Three years. Four winters.'

'And yet you still do not have the respect of the populace?' said Robin. Gisborne's eyes narrowed in irritation.

'My men and I shall leave directly for Nottingham,' he snapped.

'My servants will help you pack.'

'How was the Holy Land?' said Gisborne.

'Bloodthirsty.' Robin was not prepared to elaborate.

'I understand the King is winning.'

'He is killing more people…' Robin conceded.

'Is that not winning?'

'Show me an argument ever settled with bloodshed and then I'll call it winning.'

'Do not pretend you do not love war,' scorned Gisborne. 'I have seen you fight.'

'When?' said Robin, curious and suddenly a little more interested in the conversation.

Gisborne hesitated. 'I do not recall.'

Robin got the distinct impression he was lying. 'I have changed,' he said quietly, answering Guy's original accusation.

They were both silent for a moment.

'The Council of Nobles meets tomorrow at Nottingham.' Gisborne was businesslike again. 'I have no doubt the Sheriff will call a feast to celebrate your safe return.'

'Goodbye,' said Robin, pointedly.

'Goodbye.'

'One thing.' Robin raised his voice. 'I shall celebrate my safe return, too, by pardoning any and all wrongdoers from my estates awaiting trial or punishment.'

'Only the Sheriff can pardon, you know that,' Gisborne scorned.

'It is custom for the Sheriff to agree to his nobles' requests on such matters.'

'Then I suggest you take it up with the Sheriff,' said Gisborne, and he too stalked out of the great hall.

This was the life. Absolutely, definitely, unarguably, the life, and Much was determined it was going to be his life from now on. He lay back in the warm bath, a cosy fire roaring next to it, and reached out for his leg of pork. No more war, no more travelling, no more picking fights with the Sheriff's men and definitely no more being chased by angry fathers. He sighed happily.

The door of the oak-panelled room swung open and a serving girl entered the room carrying wood for the fire and another plate. Much covered himself hastily and put the leg of pork back. He was a gentleman now, and determined to prove it.

'Was it horrible? The war?' the girl asked him. 'What was it like?'

'War is for men,' said Much, pompously. 'You would be upset, little one.'

'Yeah?' The serving girl seemed unconvinced and far from impressed by his put-on worldliness. 'I heard dying men always ask for their mums. That,' she added, 'is for the bath.'

'What?' said Much, his mouth full.

'Rose petals.' She nodded towards the plate.

Much swallowed and looked back at the plate he'd been eating from. They did look like flowers now she came to mention it.

'I knew that,' he lied.

The girl left the room and Much was alone again. He closed his eyes. It was good to be home.

'Much, get dressed.' Robin's voice was purposeful. Much blinked – he hadn't heard the door opening. 'We are paying a visit to the old Sheriff,' said Robin, grabbing a kettle of water and starting to undress.

'Really? Is it that urgent?' said Much. He didn't like the sound of this. It was definitely more picking fights than eating in the bath.

'I forgot my promise to you,' said Robin, stopping in his tracks. He shook his head. 'You don't have to come.'

'I would prefer, I have to say, the food, bath and sleep thing,' said Much.

'Very well.' Robin disappeared behind

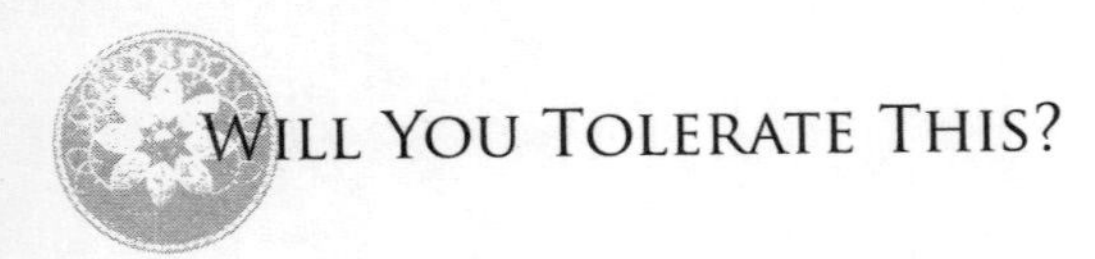

a screen to wash himself.

'Is something wrong?' Much asked.

'England is wrong,' said Robin. Over the sounds of splashing and scrubbing, Much heard the concern in his voice. 'And Nottinghamshire is worse. The old Sheriff would never have allowed this. I want to hear his story before I go to Nottingham tomorrow.'

He stepped around the screen, washed and wearing fresh clothes.

'Sleep well, my friend – you have earned it.'

Much sank back into his bath as Robin left the room. He looked over at the leg of pork. However much he wanted to, he couldn't do it. He sat up again and called after Robin. Picking a fight it was.

'I still do not see why I had to give it up,' grouched Much some time later. Their horses were nearing Knighton Hall, the home of the old Sheriff, and Much had spent most of the journey complaining.

'There will be plenty of time for eating

when we return,' Robin told him. He knew that leaving behind their homecoming feast had been near-torture for Much, but it wasn't as if the food was going to waste.

'Go into the village,' he had told Thornton before they left. 'Bring every family here and feed them. Nobody here eats until they do, including me. Those who are ill, take the food to them.'

Unfortunately, Much had overheard and, still clutching his leg of pork, felt obliged to grudgingly hand it over. He had been making his disgruntlement plain at regular intervals ever since.

Robin ignored him. The horses had slowed to a walk now, and as they passed one of the old Sheriff's outbuildings, he spotted two men lurking outside. He wondered briefly who they were, before he heard a shout.

'Get out!' It was Edward, the old Sheriff, standing wild-eyed at the front door. 'Get away from here!'

'Edward? It is me, your friend, Robin

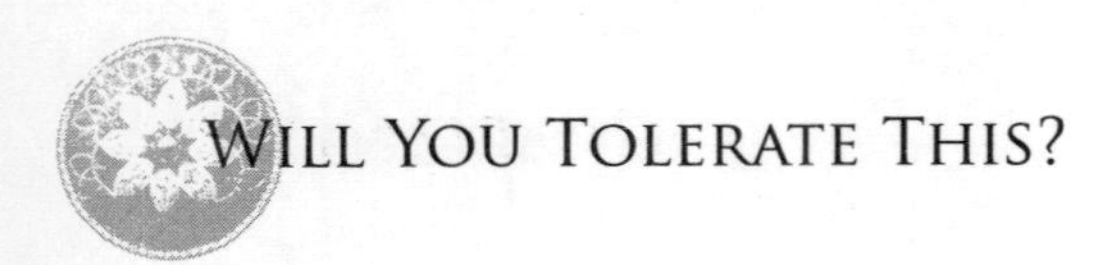

of Locksley.'

'I know who you are,' cried the old man. 'Crooks come to deceive me. Schemers! Plotters! I'll have none of you here.'

Robin was baffled by this reception. 'I swear, I come in friendship.'

'Get away!' Edward howled. 'I am no longer the Sheriff. Leave me to live out my days in peace.'

'You heard my father,' came a cool, female voice. 'Leave.'

Robin's heart leapt as Edward's daughter, Marian, emerged from the house carrying a bow. She was scowling, apparently every bit as displeased to see them as her father, but as breathtakingly beautiful as she had always been.

'Marian! It is me,' said Robin.

'Congratulations. Leave.'

'How are you? I thought of you...' Robin trailed off as she drew her bow and aimed at them.

'Leave,' she repeated.

'We are leaving,' said Much. Robin had a feeling he was remembering the fullery.

'Sir Edward,' Robin tried again, 'if you do not remember me, remember Nottingham, remember your people.' He stopped short. It was no use. Marian was already helping her father back into the house. She shot Robin and Much a last defiant look, and shut the door firmly behind her.

'Interesting,' said Robin. He could hardly believe what had just happened.

'Interesting?' Much gaped. 'Unbelievable. He used to treat us like – like sons.'

'She is still unmarried,' said Robin, dreamily.

Much breathed an 'oh' of realisation. 'I thought you had come to see the old Sheriff.'

'I did,' said Robin.

'Please.' Much looked at him, even more disgruntled than before. 'I could have remained in my bath. I could have finished my pork.'

Robin had a feeling it was going to be a long journey home.

When they eventually got back, it was to a very different scene than the one that had greeted their earlier arrival in the village. Rather than quiet desolation, a stream of people was heading slowly and happily away from the manor and back to their homes.

'Bless you, Master Robin,' one of them called out as they rode past. Robin smiled, pleased the villagers had enjoyed his feast.

'Is there food left?' Much asked the man. 'I confess, I am anxious,' he added, seeing Robin's look of reproach.

A small huddle of people nearby was laughing. Robin watched as a man in the middle of the grouped pulled faces, clowning and acting the fool to much amusement.

'Robin! Robin!' he shouted.

'Jeffrey?'

The man beamed, obviously pleased that Robin had not forgotten him.

'Remember this?' He took an egg from his pocket and regaled the crowd with a simple but showy magic trick.

'You used to love that when you were a lad,' he told Robin as the crowd around him laughed appreciatively.

'I hope you have eaten well tonight,' said Robin.

'You're a good boy. I always said.' Jeffrey nodded, and there were murmurs of agreement and thanks all around.

'That man is a show-off,' said Much as they moved onwards. 'If there are no eggs left, I'm going after him.'

Robin said nothing. The crowd thinned as they approached the manor's entrance and he saw Dan Scarlett waiting there. He was smiling, like the others, but it was a weak, strained smile and Robin knew at once something was wrong.

'What is it?' he asked.

'Young Benedict was frightened,' said Dan. 'He told Gisborne's lot who stole the flour with him.'

'Your boys?' Robin guessed.

'Gisborne and his men have taken them to

Nottingham,' said Dan and Robin saw he was fighting back tears. 'Robin...'

'I will resolve this. I will speak to the Sheriff. I promise, Dan,' said Robin, gravely. This was terrible. How could things have become so bad in the time he was away.

The more he heard about the new Sheriff, the more he wanted to meet the man and find out for himself just what was going on. Tomorrow would be an interesting day.

CHAPTER SIX

Robin had a strange sense of déjà vu riding into Nottingham the following morning. The town was much bigger than Locksley, but the uncomfortable tension, which filled the empty streets, was strikingly similar.

'Funny,' said Much looking around. 'Wednesday was always market day.'

Robin looked across at a grey-faced man standing behind a rickety pie stall.

'I think Wednesday may still be market day.'

'Surely some mistake,' said Much sceptically, as the pieman pretended he hadn't seen them.

They approached the castle gates and Robin looked up at the grand old building with growing apprehension. There were at least a dozen of the uniformed Sheriff's men standing guard and as a steward escorted him and Much inside, he could feel the atmosphere becoming tenser. As they passed through the shadow of the castle's gibbet, both Robin and Much turned their faces upwards. It looked well used.

'This way,' said the steward as they reached the stairs that led to the council chamber.

'We know the way from here, thank you,' Robin told him.

'That may be, but I am still required to see you to the chamber,' said the steward.

Robin glanced at Much, who nodded almost imperceptibly and the next moment, he dropped his pack, scattering its contents over the stone steps. The steward waited as Much scrambled around picking them up and Robin slipped past him. Arriving outside the council chamber, he pressed an ear to the door, keeping the other alert for Much and the steward.

'It has been a good month,' Robin heard someone say inside the room. 'We have collected nearly three hundred pounds and...'

A second voice, low and snide, interrupted. 'Would you want to be the King in Acre?

A clue. No. Trying to feed your army on three hundred pounds?'

There was a pause and Robin heard faint sniggering. The speaker had to be the new Sheriff, Vaizey.

'You promised five hundred,' he said.

'I – it is more than we have managed before,' came the first voice again.

'Oh, yippee,' said the Sheriff. 'The King is starving in Acre and you have failed him but,' – he adopted a mocking, girlish voice – 'it is more than we managed before.'

'…do not know how it happened,' boomed Much from the top of the stairs. Robin moved quickly away from the door and gave the steward an ingratiating smile. He looked suspicious, but said nothing.

Opening the door, he announced Robin and then backed silently out of the room.

The new Sheriff sat at the head of the table, small and wiry with cruel features and an air of unpredictability that appeared to make everyone else in the room nervous. The gathered nobles included Guy of Gisborne as well as a few other faces Robin recognised. Nottingham's priest, Canon Richard was present and so was Edward, the old Sheriff. To Robin's slight surprise, Marian stood behind her father, presumably here as his nurse.

'Locksley?' said Sheriff Vaizey. 'Welcome back. I trust Sir Guy of Gisborne managed your estates to your satisfaction?'

'I believe he may have managed them to your satisfaction,' said Robin, coolly.

'Indeed,' said the Sheriff. If he was surprised by Robin's attitude, he did not show it. 'Your peasants are unruly, by the way. We have two in custody awaiting punishment.'

'Three,' Gisborne corrected him.

'Three. Discipline will be a problem. Be warned.' The Sheriff turned away from Robin to carry on the business of the meeting. 'Loughborough?' he said to the next Lord.

'Sheriff, thank you. I can report a collection totalling...' began Lord Loughborough.

Determined to have his say, Robin interrupted.

'Discipline has never been a problem on my estates.'

'Times have changed,' snapped the Sheriff.

'Not for the better, it seems.'

'You of all people will know that the King needs funds to fight our Holy War,' said the Sheriff with a sneer.

'Is it our Holy War, or is it Pope Gregory's?' asked Robin.

'We stand shoulder to shoulder with Rome.'

'We fall shoulder to shoulder, too,' said Robin. 'I have seen it.'

The Sheriff was impatient and, Robin suspected, getting bored with a conversation he was not fully in charge of. 'That is why we need funds, and that is why we need discipline. When a populace is taxed, there is rebellion and mischief. Always a reason why this man or that man cannot pay. Always a story with sobs and heartstrings.'

'Dangerous,' said Robin. 'Keep taking and a man will eventually have nothing left to give. More to the point, nothing left to lose. Then we risk real rebellion.'

'Then what is your proposal to raise money for the King?' said the Sheriff.

'Stop all taxes,' said Robin, simply. 'Today.'

The Sheriff smirked. 'Amusing,' he said, and several of the nobles laughed.

'I do not joke,' said Robin, keeping his voice calm. 'Today is market day, and yet there is no market.'

'What is your point?' said the Sheriff.

'If a man can make more than he needs for his family, he can take what remains to market. He can trade, and the shire can take its portion. Where there is trade, there can be taxes. Until then, we must help every man – peasant, pieman, and pinner – to provide for his family. Get him trading again.'

There was a murmur around the table, and Robin sensed that there was some support for his suggestion. Instead of raging and shouting, the Sheriff lowered his voice.

'A man who can provide for his family is a comfortable man. A lazy man,' he said in a tone dripping with menace. 'He does not work. What we need is hungry men.'

He smiled around the table, his anger apparently gone as quickly as it had appeared. 'Our noble friend forgets that hungry men are virtuous.'

This time, the murmuring was in agreement with the Sheriff. Robin wondered if the nobles were missing minds of their own as well as backbones.

'Tonight there is a celebration of my return in the Great Hall,' Robin said.

'Indeed,' agreed the Sheriff.

'I trust none of us virtuous men will be feasting?'

An icy silence fell over the room and Robin knew his argument was won.

'I am unwell,' the Sheriff lied, standing up, 'so I call these proceedings, such as they are, to a halt. As the noble Lord Huntingdon remarks, there is a celebration tonight in his honour.'

'Bye,' said Robin to the Sheriff's retreating back, unable to resist a small, satisfied smile.

CHAPTER SEVEN

Will You Tolerate This?

The council drifted out of the chamber after the Sheriff, and Robin followed behind them, thinking more of what had just happened than where he was going. The new Sheriff was exactly what Robin had feared – ruthless, greedy and utterly self-interested. It was a dangerous combination. With most of his council too cowardly to stand up to him and the rest revelling in his deviousness, things looked pretty bleak for Nottingham.

Robin turned a corner, still lost in thoughts, and found himself face to face with Marian. She looked around furtively to check that they were alone.

'My father seems to think he should see you.' Her voice was quiet and matter of fact. 'His house is watched. Come there after midnight. Tonight.'

'Very well,' Robin agreed. He paused, wanting to make the most of this unexpected encounter. 'You're looking... striking. And if you still live with your father, that must mean...'

'Take care not to be seen,' she said firmly, ignoring his unspoken question.

'Don't worry. I can look after myself.'

'I don't care about you, I care about my father,' Marian snapped. 'Are you really as naïve as you seem? You think you can pick fights with these people and get away with it? You think you can slight them in public? You're a fool.'

She turned to go.

'Marian, wait.'

To Robin's slight surprise, she did as he asked. 'This is not the time, I know, but I must say, you are, more than ever,' he stumbled over the words, 'your eyes, even when you look at me in anger, I feel you, I believe you can still, after all this time...'

Robin moved closer to her and thought her expression softened. 'You can still see into my soul,' he finished.

'Five years and you're still peddling the same old drivel,' said Marian, apparently not softened at all. 'Does it ever work?'

'You'd be surprised,' said Robin.

'Amazed,' said Marian. She turned, and this time she walked away.

Robin watched her go, smiling to himself. He'd missed her. Even though she was furious with him.

Whistling softly, he started back along the corridor towards the dungeons.

Much was waiting for him when he arrived, escorted there by the steward whilst Robin had been with the council.

The jailer grunted a greeting as Robin explained who they were and what they wanted. He led them through the dank, gloomy dungeon, calling to his assistants as they went.

'Bring out the Locksley lot.'

'Hey. Hey!' called an unseen prisoner. 'That's me! Jailer!'

Robin took a seat in the jailer's cramped room

and Much stood next to him, staring warily around at the gruesome instruments of torture and punishment hanging from the walls.

The jailer reappeared a minute or two later, his odious assistants jostling three men into the room.

'Give your names,' said the jailer, pushing two of them forwards. 'Toe rag one and toe rag two.'

'Will and Luke Scarlett,' said Will, the older and bolder of the pair. Luke was pale and clearly terrified.

'What is your crime?' asked Robin.

'Living in the wrong place at the wrong time. Living under an evil sheriff. Where do our taxes go? They go to Nottingham, to the Sheriff, to his birds and his –'

A sharp blow from one of the jailer's men silenced Will's brave outburst.

The jailer ignored it. 'Name?' he said to the third prisoner.

'Benedict, son of Richard Giddens, serf, of Locksley. And my mother, Anne.'

'Benedict,' said Robin, kindly, 'what is your crime?'

'Stealing flour.'

'Are you guilty?'

Benedict's head drooped in guilty admission.

'What is your punishment?' asked Robin.

'Don't know.' Benedict shrugged.

Behind Benedict, the jailer gestured to Robin, pointing at his neck.

Much must also have seen and understood the jailer's meaning every bit as plainly as Robin. 'Hanging?' he gasped, before Robin could stop him. 'No! Surely some mistake.'

'What?' said Benedict, whipping around in panic to look from the jailer, to Much, and then back to Robin. 'What? Hanging? No! No!'

Luke Scarlett ran to Robin. 'Robin, save us! Dad said you would save us!'

The jailer's face was thunderous. He waved to his men, who each caught hold of a prisoner and dragged the three of them back to their cells.

'Please,' called Benedict over his shoulder, 'I beg you, I beg you.'

'Do you mind?' said the disgruntled jailer, turning on Much. 'We don't tell 'em if it's the dangle – they kick up a stink.'

Much was not cowed. 'For stealing flour – hanging?' he demanded. Robin couldn't have put it better himself.

The jailer jerked his head upwards, indicating the higher levels of the castle. 'Sheriff wants an example,' he said. 'Just had word.'

'I will be speaking to the Sheriff,' said Robin. 'Meanwhile, treat these prisoners well, or you will have me to answer to.'

The jailer scowled, but didn't answer. Robin stood up to leave and Much, more than glad to be getting out of the depressing little room, made to follow.

'You've got one more,' said the jailer, ducking out of the room. He reappeared a moment later with the man Robin and Much had rescued in the forest a few days earlier.

'You're not from Locksley,' said Robin

in surprise.

'I know. But you saved me once before.' As the man spoke, Robin realised it was his voice which had called out as they passed the cells.

'That was a long way from Nottingham,' Robin said. 'Here I am known.'

'You're saving those others,' the man reasoned. 'You'll save me. For my wife, my newborn babe. Please.'

'You said your wife was expecting,' Much pointed out, suspiciously.

'She had the baby,' said the man. Much looked at the man doubtfully.

'Your lies today may be your undoing,' said Robin. 'I cannot save the others, and now I fear you may share their fate.'

'What fate?'

Robin turned to leave again without replying. He did not want to repeat Much's earlier mistake. If this man was to be hung, surely it was better he did not live his last day in terror at the prospect.

Unfortunately, the jailer's grim face must

have given the game away, because as Much and Robin left, they heard the man shouting.

'I'm not from Locksley. Did I say Locksley? There's been a mistake. I'm from Rochdale. Rochdale! That's why they call me Allan A Dale!'

'Yeah, and I'm from wild Wales,' the jailer said. 'Put 'im in with the Locksley lot. They can whine together tonight and swing together in the morning.'

Allan A Dale's shouting faded as Robin and Much walked quickly along the corridor and out of the dungeons. Robin's face was as grimly determined as the jailer's. He may not be able to do anything about the whining, but if he could help it, there would be no one swinging in the morning.

CHAPTER EIGHT

WILL YOU TOLERATE THIS?

'It's definitely swan,' said Much as they arrived in the Great Hall later that evening. Judging by the noise coming from inside, the celebration feast in honour of Robin's return was already in full swing. Much was sniffing the air, trying to guess what they might be eating.

'I thought at first, it was duck, but now I am certain it is roast swan. It smells...' he sniffed the air again, 'bigger than duck. And much tastier.'

Robin wasn't paying attention. Instead of heading through the vast carved wooden doors, which led into the Great Hall, he veered off to one side. Much watched him for a moment and quickly saw where Robin was headed; the new Sheriff was outside the Hall talking to Gisborne. With a last, longing sniff of swan, Much followed Robin, catching up as he tapped

SheriffVaizey on the shoulder.

'Huntingdon,' the Sheriff said, turning around. 'You've been missing your own feast. Rumours abound.'

'What rumours?'

'That you are weak,' said the Sheriff. 'You've come back weakened after your exertions in the Holy Land. I hear you were wounded...?'

Much bristled. 'My master returns with honours, honours from the King...' he began, but Robin placed a hand lightly on his shoulder to silence him.

'The greater honour is to stay and fight beside him, surely?' the Sheriff taunted.

As far as Much was concerned, this rude, disrespectful, rat-like little man was asking for a hiding, and Robin seemed like just the man to give it to him. But Robin ignored the Sheriff's words and instead steered the conversation towards more pressing matters.

'I have visited my peasants in your dungeons.'

'You have four, not three, I gather,' said

the Sheriff.

'They have committed grave crimes,' Robin admitted.

Much was indignant. The hiding was definitely a better plan than this. 'Master, surely –' he said, but Robin interrupted again.

'Which would make all the more compassionate your gesture of pardoning them.'

'Pardoning them?' sneered Vaizey. 'I will see them hanged in the morning. You said yourself we risk rebellion. We must have order. A little fear is useful.'

'It is custom for the Sheriff to hear his nobles' requests for charity and favour,' Robin persisted.

'La dee dah dee dah,' mocked the Sheriff.

Much ground his teeth.

'In your absence,' the Sheriff continued, looking Robin straight in the eye, 'we nominated you to oversee the morning's entertainments.'

'No,' said Robin, flatly.

'You don't want these rumours of weakness to spread. Stop them now, or we'll all pay.'

And with that, the Sheriff turned and strode off into the party.

In his place, Marian appeared, also on her way to the Great Hall. Much looked at Robin, expecting him to throw out one of his well-practised lines, but it was Gisborne who spoke first.

'Marian – might I have the pleasure of your company?'

A tiny flicker of hesitation crossed her face, and then she nodded politely and allowed him to take her arm. As they walked away, Gisborne turned round and threw Robin a painfully false smile.

Much was so angry, he almost forgot the roast swan.

CHAPTER NINE

Will You Tolerate This?

Robin knocked on the back door of Knighton Hall. Beside him, Much shivered in the chilly night air. It was past midnight and Robin was as sure as he could be that no one had seen them arrive. The door opened quickly, but seeing Marian there in front of him, Robin hesitated.

'Don't just stand there,' she scolded. 'If the Sheriff's people see…'

'What? You might give them the pleasure of your company?'

'Grow up,' said Marian.

She led them into the house, hardly looking at Robin as the three of them made their way to the sitting room. How things had changed for Marian and her father, now that he was no longer the Sheriff of Nottingham. Gone were the comforts and luxuries of their old life. Knighton Hall was nothing compared to their former home. They felt like exiles here.

Marian's father was waiting for them, and he greeted Robin and Much in turn. Robin was pleased and rather relieved to see Edward was more his old self than the man they had encountered on their last visit.

'Forgive me,' said Edward. 'I could not welcome you before.'

'How did this monster become Sheriff?' asked Robin, keen to get straight to the point at this late hour.

'I did not watch my back. Prince John gives out the shires in his brother's absence. My bid was not accepted.'

'What can be done?'

'I can do nothing,' Edward confessed. 'I am watched, and I must think of my daughter. When I do speak out, no one listens. I'm yesterday's news. Robin, it is down to you my friend.'

'What can we do?' said Much.

Robin was grateful yet again for his friend's

loyalty. We're a team Much seemed to be reminding him. You won't be doing this on your own.

'Play Nottingham's game,' Edward said. 'Speak to the lords. Slowly you can turn them. Do not make the mistake I and others have made and make your dissent public. Reinforce your position quietly.'

'I do not have time. Tomorrow I am to order the hanging of four of my own peasants,' said Robin.

Edward shrugged, sadly. 'It will be the long game, I'm afraid.'

'Will and Luke Scarlett cannot wait,' Robin argued. 'Benedict Giddens. Allan A Dale.'

'You must let them go,' said Marian. Robin had a feeling she'd been dying to chip in to the conversation. 'It is a test. Fail it and there will be consequences.'

'Perhaps…' said Robin.

'Definitely. This is not a ga–'

Marian fell silent at the warning look on her father's face.

'My daughter speaks when she should not,' he said, gently. 'But she is right. You have no choice, Robin. Hide your temper. Bide your time until you can act decisively, or kiss your lands, if not your life, goodbye.'

The old Sheriff's words rang in Robin's ears as he sat at home much later that night.

He knew Edward's advice made sense. Marian agreed with him and from the conversation they'd had on the way home, it appeared Much did, too.

'I am sorry for the Scarlett lads, me,' Much had said. 'Good boys. And young Giddens. Harsh.'

'Harsh?' Robin had echoed. 'It is ungodly. I thought we were fighting for God and justice. The Turk knows both better.'

'True. But you heard the old Sheriff. It is their lives or your land. Their lives or our lives.'

'I swore after the Holy Land I would have no further hand in bloodshed,' said Robin.

'This is not war,' Much reminded him.

'This is the law.'

'It is war, between state and serf,' said Robin.

'And anyway, their lives are not worth so much.'

'Much!'

'They aren't,' Much protested. 'They are poor. They will never know comfort. They are miserable. They have suffered. It will be a kindness to end it for them now. It will be a mercy.'

But however much he valued Edward's advice or Much's opinion, Robin could not see the Scarlett boys and Benedict Giddens put to death. Even Allan A Dale had done nothing worthy of hanging. If he saved the four of them, was he really condemning the whole of Nottingham to an equally dreadful fate in the long run? He bowed his head, resting its weight in his hands. If it took all night, he had to make a decision, and then make a plan.

CHAPTER TEN

Will You Tolerate This?

The courtyard at Nottingham Castle was transformed when Robin and Much arrived the following morning. The crowds may have stayed away on market day, but although the villagers and townspeople hated public executions, they gathered now with a sense of trepidation, with a morbid fear that they might be the next to 'swing'. A hangman, who was busy checking four ropes that dangled ominously from the crosspiece, now staffed the gibbet they had walked beneath the previous day. As they made their way through the crowd, a woman spat in disgust at Robin.

'Murderer!' she called after him.

Robin ignored her. He had just caught sight of Dan Scarlett amongst a group of villagers he recognised from Locksley. He tried to disappear back into the crowd before they spotted him – he could think of nothing to say to Will and Luke's father – but it was too late. Dan strode over to greet Robin and Much.

'Dan...'

'Robin, it's not your fault,' said Dan, and Robin felt a fresh wave of guilt and dread wash over him. A man so reasonable and good-hearted should not be in Dan Scarlett's position.

He was saved from offering hollow words of consolation by a showy fanfare of trumpets, which announced the arrival of the Sheriff. Vaizey was dressed in full regalia and followed by Canon Richard, the weak, fawning council members and Edward with Marian, as usual, at his side. Robin allowed himself a few seconds to marvel at how beautiful she looked, even on a day like today. Her dress was simple but elegant, and her dark hair was piled into an elaborately adorned headdress.

'Lords, ladies, people of Nottingham,' began the Sheriff in his quiet, lazy drawl, and Robin pulled his eyes away from Marian. 'We are here today to witness the carrying out of justice in the name of God and King Richard.'

He turned to order his men-at-arms. 'Bring out the prisoners.'

Will and Luke Scarlett, Benedict Giddens and Allan A Dale were each led out to stand on a stool beneath one of the four ropes. The hangman eyed them eagerly.

'Robin of Locksley, Earl of Huntingdon, recently returned from the Holy Land with a personal commendation from the King himself will read the proclamation,' announced the Sheriff. He handed Robin a scroll and dropped his voice so the crowd could not hear. 'Enjoy,' he said, smugly. 'And, uh, in case you have any second thoughts, your friend Much will be dropping in as our special guest today.'

He cast an unconvincingly casual glance towards the castle battlements and with a feeling of dread, Robin followed the direction of his gaze. There, high above the stone courtyard was Much. He was flanked by two of the Sheriff's most enormous men, each gripping him rigidly so he stood teetering on the edge of the narrow parapet. Robin's heart sank. How had he become so distracted that he didn't notice these oafs capture Much? He took one last look at the fearful, apologetic expression on Much's face and then opened the scroll. He had no choice.

'Let it be heard and known across the lands and realms of His Majesty, Richard, King of England,' Robin read, his voice toneless and defeated, 'that on this, the 26th day of April, in the year of our Lord eleven hundred and ninety-two, the following men, having been tried under law, and found guilty. Benedict Giddens of Locksley, Luke Scarlett of Locksley, Will Scarlett of Locksley, Allan A Dale of Locksley. These same men have been sentenced to hang by a rope until they are dead.'

The hangman watched him in anticipation and Robin nodded reluctantly. His stomach churned unpleasantly as his villagers and Allan A Dale were all, in turn, blindfolded. The hangman placed a noose around each neck and a drum began beating ominously. Robin caught sight of the Sheriff. He was quietly imitating each sombre drumbeat and clearly enjoying the whole spectacle. The drummer stood a short way behind him and for a moment, Robin was distracted.

'That drum is from the Holy Land.'

'Yes,' the Sheriff agreed. 'A tabor. Good, eh?' And he nodded across to Guy of Gisborne. Robin frowned. Did he mean the drum had been a gift from Gisborne?

'Rare in these parts.' Robin pressed, but they were interrupted by a shout.

'Wait! Wait!'

The Sheriff raised his eyebrows as if unsurprised by this last minute disruption. 'Nah, nah, nah,' he mocked, 'don't kill my lovely boy, my baby, my –'

But as the crowd parted to let the speaker through, it wasn't a wailing parent, but a priest who stepped forward. He gestured for silence and the drum stopped. Robin swallowed nervously.

'On behalf of Anthony, our bishop, I claim benefit of clergy for these men,' the Priest announced. 'They cannot hang.'

'These are not holy men,' said the Sheriff, dismissively. 'They cannot plead the cloth.' He turned to Robin. 'Get on with it.'

'I came last night to administer their last rites,' the Priest persisted.

The Sheriff looked to the jailer for confirmation. The jailer shrugged and inclined his head in a 'yes'.

'So?' The Sheriff snapped.

'And each one came to God through me, repenting his sins, and asking to take the cloth,' said the Priest. 'I felt duty-bound to consult the Bishop, and he in turn confers status of novice onto each man.'

He unravelled a scroll and began to read aloud.

'I, Anthony, Very Reverend Vicar Apostolic, hereby confer–'

'Shut up,' said the Sheriff. He turned to Canon Richard. 'Is this possible?'

'They could not become novices overnight,' the Canon said.

'They are become Postulants,' explained the Priest. 'Novice novices, if you like, and so are under the protection of the church.'

The Sheriff fell silent. Robin's heart pounded in his chest. Was it going to work? The Priest – the not-at-all-reverend Jeffrey, joker, actor and by Much's reckoning, show-off, of Locksley – caught his eye and Robin quickly looked away. The Sheriff must not suspect anything.

'Novice novices?' said the Sheriff slowly, looking from Robin to Jeffrey and then back again. 'How novel.'

Too late, realised Robin. The game was up.

'Hang 'em,' snarled the Sheriff. He pointed at Jeffrey in his borrowed Priest's robes. 'And arrest him.'

Jeffrey bolted, but the men-at-arms were too fast for him. The nearest one grabbed at him, ripping off the goatee beard which disguised his face. Undeterred, Jeffrey carried on running, weaving his way through the crowd, but it was no good. A moment later, another of the Sheriff's man caught up with him and the chase was over. Jeffrey gave Robin a look of apology over his shoulder as the men-at-arms led him roughly away towards the castle dungeons.

'Where's the drum?' said the Sheriff, sounding almost gleeful now.

Robin took a deep breath as the ominous pounding started up again. He was quickly running out of options.

'May the souls of these men find forgiveness in heaven,' the Sheriff parroted, obviously keen to finish the proceedings without further interruption. He nodded to the eager hangman.

His moment finally arrived, the hangman kicked away the stool beneath each prisoner with a well-practised foot.

The crowd gasped and the slow drumbeat became a frantic, breathless roll as the four ropes tautened.

Robin heard Benedict Giddens' mother scream, saw the look of despair on Dan Scarlett's face and yet again, wondered that things in Nottingham had come to this.

'Watch and enjoy.' The Sheriff sneered, leaning in close to enjoy Robin's horror. 'The Priest will talk. Then you will be done for, my friend.'

CHAPTER ELEVEN

Will You Tolerate This?

As the Sheriff walked away, Robin looked around desperately. He could not, would not, stand here and watch four undeserving men die. If his plans hadn't worked, he'd just have to improvise. Two of the men-at-arms standing guard around the Sheriff were archers, both with bow in hand and quiver behind. Taking his chance, Robin tapped one on the shoulder. The archer turned round and then dropped heavily to the floor as Robin punched him square in the face. He snatched up the man's bow, grimacing as he tested the cheap and nasty strings, and whipped four fresh arrows from the quiver.

Standing up and raising the bow, Robin spoke loudly and clearly to the crowd as he took aim.

'People of Nottingham.'

He fired. The arrow found its target and sliced through the rope above Luke Scarlett's head.

'These men have committed no crime worth more than a spell in the stocks.'

A second arrow split the next rope, and Robin fired a third. Will Scarlett and Benedict Giddens fell to the ground, released.

'Will you tolerate this injustice? I, for one,' proclaimed Robin as his fourth and final arrow pierced Allan A Dale's rope, 'will not.'

The crowd roared their approval, those nearest the four freed men clamouring to help them remove their blindfolds and bindings.

Robin lowered his bow. He knew he had just sealed his own fate, but he was equally certain he had done the right thing.

From his precarious viewpoint high above the castle courtyard, Much watched, barely noticing his brutish captors as the scene below turned to chaos. The Sheriff's men swarmed at Robin, but Much knew he had faced worse odds and enemies. Instead of running away from them, Robin headed straight at the oncoming mob, tucking in his arms and legs as he rolled into a somersault. The men were sent flying in all directions and Much just had time to see Robin grab a sword from one of them before he realised his own situation had changed. The guards on either side of him had taken a firmer hold on his arms and before Much could protest, his feet were lifted over the edge of the battlements. If the narrow stone ledge had been terrifying, it was nothing to the vast drop which was now directly beneath his boots.

From the courtyard, the Sheriff smirked up at him. The men were obviously acting on his instruction, and Robin, now engaged in a fresh battle with his stolen sword, appeared to have just noticed what was happening. Much said a silent prayer. If ever he'd needed Robin's brand of reckless but brilliant bravery, it was now.

'Master!' he yelled. 'Help!'

'Yield, Locksley,' said the Sheriff as Robin

froze, staring up at the dangling, struggling figure of his friend, 'or say farewell to your little Mulch.'

'His name is Much.' Robin hissed.

'He'll be Mulch in a moment,' the Sheriff scoffed, and lifted his hand to make a 'drop him' signal at the two men who held Much's life in their loutish hands.

But Robin wasn't about to be beaten now. Moving faster than the lazy, cavalier Sheriff, he gripped the stolen sword, gathered every ounce of his strength and threw it upwards. It soared towards the guards on the battlements, as accurate as his arrows had been just a few minutes earlier. Hitting first one tin-helmeted head and then the other, it knocked Much's captors backwards and he fell with them, safely onto the castle roof. Robin watched as Much struggled free and stood up, not sure who was more elated by his lucky escape.

All around Robin, people were still fighting. Allan A Dale battled one of the men-at-arms, Will Scarlett had just freed Jeffrey in his now-torn priest's robes from the men who had been holding him captive, and Robin saw Luke Scarlett reunited with his father. This was more like it, thought Robin. People were standing up to the Sheriff and finally fighting back.

'Master! Look out!' cried a voice.

It was Much again. Robin spun round and found himself face to face with the Sheriff's other archer. This one was fully conscious and still in possession of his cheap, nasty but nonetheless effective bow. What was more, it was drawn and pointing directly at Robin. He had given up his sword to save Much, there were no more arrows left in his quiver and standing this close, there was no hope that even the worst archer would miss him.

The archer looked to the Sheriff who nodded his permission to fire. Vaizey's delight at this turn of events was as plain as the beard on his smug face. Turning back to Robin, the archer took aim but then, without warning, staggered sideways. Robin stared as the man recoiled, apparently in agony and it took a moment before he worked out what was causing it. Newly embedded in his left arm was a jewelled dagger. Robin looked around, confused. Someone must have thrown it, but who?

A short distance away, Marian was being ushered towards the castle by her father and as she looked back at Robin, he spotted something glittering in her hair. It seemed unlikely, impossible even, but there, tucked into Marian's headdress was a single hairpin, bejewelled, and identical to the dagger protruding from the archer's arm. On the other side of her head, where its twin should have been, there was nothing, which must mean...

Robin blinked, thinking he might be imagining it, but when he opened his eyes, there was still only one hairpin there in her headdress. He gazed quizzically at Marian, and received a stinging, withering look in reply. It didn't matter, though. She had saved him.

'This way!' Jeffrey was gesturing to Robin from a door at the side of the courtyard. Will, Allan and Much, fresh from his rooftop escape, were waiting there, clearly agitated and keen to get away.

Robin took one last, disbelieving look at Marian.

'Robin!' shouted Much, exasperated.

Snapping out of his reverie, Robin dashed across to join them, leaving a thwarted and greatly disappointed Sheriff to fume.

CHAPTER TWELVE

The streets outside were buzzing with news of what had just happened in the castle courtyard. Everywhere he looked and at every stall they ran past, Much saw people gossiping, heard snatches of stories and rumours being swapped. With Robin leading the way, Will Scarlett and Allan A Dale behind him, Much ran onwards through the familiar street, unsure of where they would end up. He suspected Robin didn't know either, but he had got them this far and Much knew from long experience that it was best just to trust him. Ahead, Robin made a sudden turn and disappeared. Much cast around, trying to see where he'd gone. He glimpsed a group of Sheriff's men coming towards them, just as he spotted the alleyway Robin had ducked into. Much piled in behind him, and the others joined them a second later. Leaning against the cool stone of the alley walls, breathing heavily, they waited as the sound of running footfalls approached and then passed by. Allan had been the last to slip into the alleyway, and he was nearest to the street outside. As the footsteps faded he went to step back out into the bustling market. Anticipating what he was about to do, Much grabbed his cloak and stopped him just in time. A lone Sheriff's man strode past the end of the alley, his black cloak whipped by the breeze as he made a final check of the marketplace.

'The last man!' Much whispered to Allan in an admonishing tone. 'Don't you know anything?'

'Come on,' said Robin, edging past them and peering out to check the coast was clear. Much, Will and Allan followed him into the street and then stood behind him waiting. Much guessed that the others, like him, were hoping Robin had a plan, or some inspired suggestion as to what they should do, where they should go now. He was quiet for a few moments, taking in the street around him. Much watched as Robin's gaze finally settled on a narrow passage directly opposite the alleyway they'd been hiding in. It was dark and dingy, but as Much's eyes adjusted to the gloom, he made out what Robin had obviously seen, too – a pair of black horses, un-tethered and looking as much like an escape plan as anything Much had ever seen. Robin turned round and grinned, jerking his head towards the passage and then sprinted off across the marketplace. Much, Will and Allan followed and a moment later, emerged back onto the street, heading for the city gates, two to a horse.

As they rode, Robin felt his heart thumping faster. They were so close now. Once outside the city, he'd need a new plan, but at least they would be away from the immediate danger of the Sheriff and his men. That alone would make it easier for Robin to think.

All around them, the crowds still chattered

and shouted, passing on news of events at the castle.

'...an arrow, right through the ropes!' he heard someone exclaim.

'Never seen the like,' called someone else to his neighbour as they passed.

'Shut the gates!' came a cry, and not a minute later, the same thing again. 'Shut the gates!'

But it was too late. Robin and Much, on the first horse, came galloping past the guard. He stumbled back against the gatepost, as Robin spurred his horse forwards. Turning to make sure the others were still following, Robin saw Allan A Dale swing out a leg as the second horse passed the guard. He fell clumsily into the mud and all four fugitives clattered through the city gates and out onto the drawbridge.

At the far end of the bridge, a fresh mob of guards manned a checkpoint, another gate. The guards outnumbered them and they stood waiting for action, bows at the ready. As Robin took in the situation, one of the men began to lower the checkpoint gate. They were trapped.

Robin surveyed the scene, taking everything in and thinking fast. The best thing to do with a problem was to face it head on. Just because your problem was a hoard of armed guards didn't mean you couldn't deal with it in the same way. He kicked his heels against the horse's girth. There was only one thing to do. Decision made, and with a rush of exhilaration, he rode straight at the checkpoint. A volley of arrows rained around them as the guards sprang into action. Robin felt Much tense behind him and knew his friend was terrified. He kept going, his eyes fixed on the other side of the gate. Much would be fine. They would all be fine. Arrows rushed past, coming from all directions, but none of them found flesh. Through the adrenaline which pounded in his ears, Robin heard the faint sounds of guards shouting and as they reached the end of the drawbridge, he saw the men throwing themselves out of the horses' path. He kept riding, through the gate and over the end of the bridge with the second horse close behind. They were free, all four of them. Safe and unscathed, for now at least.

Robin leaned low over the horse's mane as they sped away across open countryside. What their future was, he did not know. He could not go back to Locksley Manor, that much was certain. He was a wanted man, an outlaw, and his fate if the Sheriff caught him would be the same as that of the men he had just saved. But a new life might not be so bad. A fresh start. Nothing like the life he had known before leaving England, or since, but better than a life under this Sheriff's tyrannical and unjust laws.

'Where are we going?' called Much from behind.

Robin grinned.

'Sherwood Forest!' he shouted back, and pulling up his hood against the stinging wind, he spurred the horse on towards their new home.